MUSEUM MYSTERY SQUAD

TOP SECRET
★ ★ ★

To Dalkeith Library,
where I began reading mysteries – M.N.

To Layla – M.P.

Kelpies is an imprint of Floris Books
First published in 2017 by Floris Books
Text © 2017 Mike Nicholson. Illustrations © 2017 Floris Books
Mike Nicholson and Mike Phillips have asserted their rights
under the Copyright, Designs and Patent Act 1988
to be identified as the Author and Illustrator of this work

The publisher acknowledges subsidy from
Creative Scotland towards the publication
of this volume

British Library CIP data available
ISBN 978-178250-361-3
Printed & bound by MBM Print SCS Ltd, Glasgow

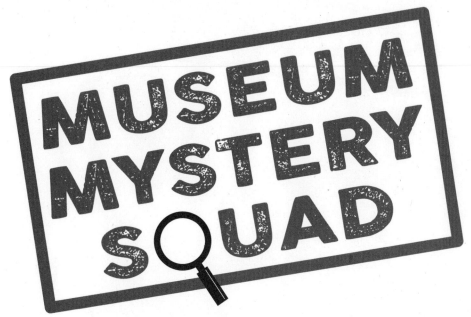

MUSEUM MYSTERY SQUAD

and the Case of the
Moving Mammoth

Written by Mike Nicholson

Illustrated by Mike Phillips

Young Kelpies

THE SQUAD

Kennedy

Nabster

Laurie

Colin the hamster

Magda Gaskar

Gus

AND FEATURING...

Tyrone O'Saurus

Moth

PREHISTORIC ANIMALS!

PTERODACTYL

SABRE-TOOTHED TIGER

TYRANNOSAURUS REX

BRONTOSAURUS

TRICERATOPS

STEGOSAURUS

PLESIOSAUR

ARCHAEOPTERYX

MAMMOTH

Some people think that museums are boring places.

Glass cases. Old stuff. Dust.

Wrong.

Think more of

wild animals

ANCIENT MUMMIES

enormous insects

COLOURFUL COSTUMES

glittering treasure

and amazing objects found nowhere else in the world.

Then imagine that each thing in the museum has its own strange story. With secrets from the past to be uncovered. Codes to be cracked. Odd characters and their fiendish plans. Each one creating a job for a team of expert investigators:

MUSEUM MYSTERY SQUAD

In this book you will find the Squad in the depths of the museum, somewhere in a maze of corridors and stairs.

Today, like every day, they have a puzzle to solve...

Chapter 1
In which a hamster does backflips and dinosaurs come to town

Colin was doing acrobatics. He swung, he rolled, he clambered! His small furry body bounced like a brown tennis ball. It was a hamster gymnastic display.

He seemed to be copying the action on the enormous interactive screen. An acrobat on a trapeze was performing incredible spins in the air.

"I think Colin's inspired because there's a circus in town." Nabster had switched on the news.

Kennedy looked up from her diary, and Laurie climbed into his usual position (inside his sleeping bag on the sofa). Along with Nabster (or Mohammed McNab as he was really called), they were the museum's team of expert investigators: the Museum Mystery Squad. Whenever there was a secret to uncover or strange stories to investigate, the museum director, Magda Gaskar, turned to them.

"It looks a bit of an odd circus." Nabster gazed at the huge screen, which took up most of one wall of their headquarters. The news pictures showed an enormous tent. No great surprise for a circus. But the door into it was no ordinary tent flap. It was a giant bone archway. And all of the lorries and vans parked around were painted with pictures of roaring dinosaurs.

"Yes, we've got the

in town," said Kennedy Kerr, checking the calendar. Kennedy was often a step ahead of everyone else, spotting and organising vital information. On many of the Museum Mystery Squad's cases she made the connections that solved the mysteries. Kennedy was also usually an *actual* step ahead of everyone else. She not only thought quickly, she moved fast too. When they were out and about, her teammates just managed to keep sight of her frizzy ginger hair in the distance.

Kennedy was a winning combination: hyper-brainy, mega-organised and super-fast.

"Dinosaur Circus?" said Laurie. "How does that work if dinosaurs are extinct?"

Asking the question everyone else was thinking was Laurie Lennox's great skill. He seemed laid back to the point of being lazy, spending much of his time in a sleeping bag on the sofa. Even his fringe flopped over his eyes as if it couldn't be bothered. But it was often a simple direct question from Laurie that moved the

Squad's investigations on in giant leaps, and got to the heart of the mystery. Laurie really looked at things. When he gazed at you through his big black-framed glasses, you felt as though you were being x-rayed for the truth.

Anyone meeting Laurie for the first time wanted to ask the same question: Why do you wear such weird clothes? Today he was dressed in:

 baseball boots (fair enough)

 an army jacket (slightly strange)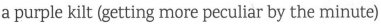

a purple kilt (getting more peculiar by the minute)

and a top hat (really?!!)

This was not an unusual outfit for Laurie. His wardrobe rail beside the sofa in the Squad HQ looked like a fancy dress shop in the middle of a science lab.

If anyone did actually ask Laurie why he wore unusual clothes, he answered with a question: "Why not?" He did things just the way he wanted to, and somehow always looked cool – in a Laurie Lennox way.

"It's a 'circus with a prehistoric twist'," said Nabster. Information was scrolling across the TV screen beside images of clowns and a highwire. "Circus acts with a fun link to a fearsome past," he read.

In the Museum Mystery Squad's headquarters, Nabster could always be found in front of the laptop, searching the internet and delving into the Squad's files and databases. He would stream any information he found onto the wall screen for the others to see. On his wrist he wore a watch-sized version of his laptop, giving him access to investigation files wherever the Squad went.

Every team needs a technical expert and in the Museum Mystery Squad it was Mohammed McNab. The Nabster. Not only was he a huge fan of using gadgets, from iPods to cake mixers and hair driers, he would also happily take them all apart. Then, joining them back together, he would make something completely new, like the iPod cake drier, which plays music while baking something tasty. Genius. With pieces of wire and pliers sticking out of his pocket, Nabster was always ready to create something new.

So there you have it: the story of what lay behind a battered metal door in a remote corridor deep underneath the museum. The sign on the door said

M.M.S.

and inside was The Museum Mystery Squad – Kennedy Kerr, Laurie Lennox, and Nabster. And one other member of the team: Colin the hamster.

Colin didn't say a lot (a bit like other hamsters) and his keyboard skills were pretty poor (much like most small furry creatures). His occasional jogs across Nabster's laptop always got the same result:

gobbledygook. However, Colin had a knack for giving the team ideas that helped them solve cases, so they let him off for being a bit smelly and needing his straw changed every week.

Nabster continued to tap at the keyboard. Kennedy made notes as information and images flew around the screen. Laurie lazed on the sofa but expertly tossed his top hat onto a hook on the wall. "So this Dinosaur Circus," he said, "do they have a T-rex on a tightrope?"

As he spoke, Colin tried to walk along a tiny ladder in his cage and fell off into his straw.

Meanwhile, upstairs in the museum, another animal had toppled over too, but only one person had noticed.

So far.

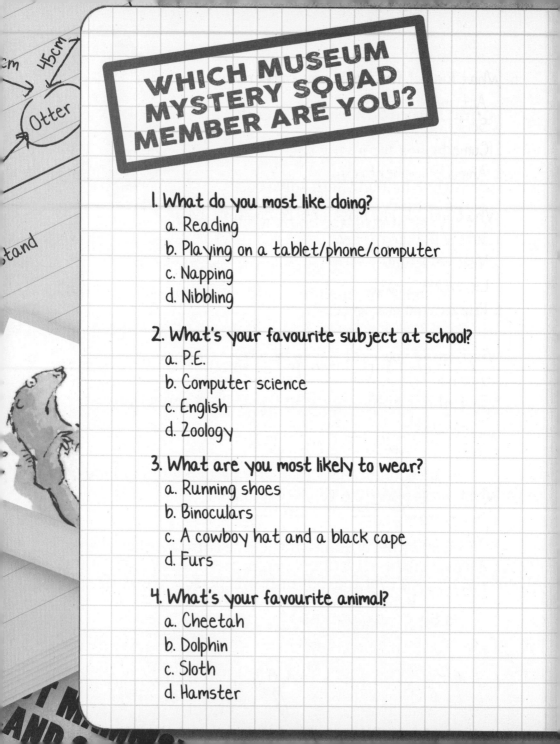

WHICH MUSEUM MYSTERY SQUAD MEMBER ARE YOU?

1. What do you most like doing?
a. Reading
b. Playing on a tablet/phone/computer
c. Napping
d. Nibbling

2. What's your favourite subject at school?
a. P.E.
b. Computer science
c. English
d. Zoology

3. What are you most likely to wear?
a. Running shoes
b. Binoculars
c. A cowboy hat and a black cape
d. Furs

4. What's your favourite animal?
a. Cheetah
b. Dolphin
c. Sloth
d. Hamster

5. What kind of film would you rather watch?
- a. Action/adventure
- b. Sci-Fi
- c. Comedy
- d. Animal documentary

6. What would you most like to do on holiday?
- a. White-water rafting
- b. Visit museums
- c. Lie on the beach
- d. Run around in a wheel

7. What would you most like to be when you grow up?
- a. Author
- b. Inventor
- c. Journalist
- d. Just the same as you are now

8. What would you take to a desert island?
- a. Your diary
- b. Your favourite gadget
- c. A sleeping bag
- d. Carrots

Colin

ANSWERS ON THE LAST PAGE

Chapter 2
In which animals are reported to be on the move

Nabster soon confirmed that the

was in fact a circus *without* dinosaurs.

Yes there were a lot of pictures of dinosaurs on the lorries and vans.

Sure enough the archway into the circus tent was a giant jawbone.

Without a doubt there were recorded roars echoing from loudspeakers around the circus tent in the Meadows.

But... the number of *actual* dinosaurs appearing was exactly:

Zero.
Zip.
Zilch.

= 0

There were, however, a lot of dinosaur names squeezed into the list of performers.

"Terri Dactyl the Trapeze Girl," said Kennedy, reading through the acts on offer.

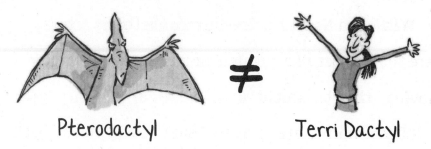

Pterodactyl ≠ Terri Dactyl

"Archie Opteryx the Highwire Hero," said Nabster.

Archaeopteryx ≠ Archie Opteryx

"Sabrina the Sabre-Toothed Tiger Tamer?" said Kennedy. She looked closely at the picture. "Those are very fake fangs."

"Any clowns? I like clowns," said Laurie, starting to thread some new rainbow laces into his baseball boots.

"Yes," said Nabster. "The Bronto Brothers. It says here they're just like a couple of brontosauruses: slow moving and a bit stupid."

"These names are so awful," said Laurie. He lay back on the sofa again. "I need a rest."

"Wait till you hear what the ringmaster and circus manager is called," said Kennedy, "Tyrone O'Saurus." A picture came up on the screen of a large man in a bright checked jacket.

Laurie groaned and pulled the sleeping bag over his head to avoid any more painful dinosaur puns.

"According to this report, the circus being in Edinburgh is big news for the museum. They might not have dinosaurs, but they have brought Moth with them," said Nabster.

"A moth? How much excitement can that bring? A moth is not exactly a crowd-puller," said Laurie's muffled voice from inside the sleeping bag.

"Moth is not *a moth*," said Kennedy.

Moth ≠

"As long as the circus is here she's being looked after right under this roof. Loads of people have been coming to see her."

A new photo of a very different creature appeared on the screen.

"Who's Moth?" asked the still-invisible Laurie.

"You can see her upstairs in the Animal Zone," said Nabster winking at Kennedy.

"Yes, but *who is she?*" The lump on the sofa now sounded cross.

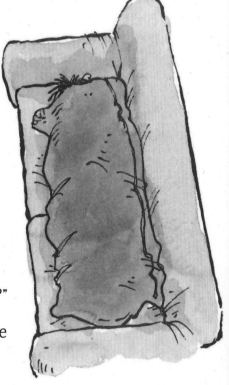

"She'll be here for three days," said Kennedy, grinning and reading off the screen.

"Do you have a number I can call her on to ask her *who she is?*" asked the still-hidden Laurie. "Since you two think it's such a secret."

PING! The sound of an email arriving was the only answer Laurie got.

"Perfect timing. Here's your chance to meet Moth," said Nabster, reading the message. "We have a new case. We need to check out Moth and some of her Animal Zone pals."

To: **MMS@museums.co.uk**
Subject: Museum Mystery Squad – Investigation Required

Dear Kennedy, Laurence and Mohammed,
I'd like you to take a look at this.
I got this message from Bea Menzies, the Animal Zone's cleaner:
Something very odd is happening. I've had a great shock.
The stuffed animals are moving at night. I promise it's true!
We need to take extra care while Moth is here, so can you please investigate?
Thank you as ever,
Magda Gaskar
Museum Director

That got Laurie out of his sleeping bag. He sat up and looked at the others.

"How can a stuffed animal move?" he asked. "Stuffed animals are dead. Dead things don't move. End of."

"I thought you were stuffed and unable to move a minute ago," said Nabster, quickly typing a reply to the museum director.

"Maybe they've just been poked by a passerby?" said Kennedy. "People love to touch things in the museum."

"Yes, it's amazing how tempting it is when there's a sign saying **PLEASE DO NOT TOUCH**," said Nabster.

"But the email said it had happened at night, so there wouldn't be anyone here," said Laurie.

"The cleaners arrive early in the morning," said Nabster. "Maybe a hoover has thumped into the animals."

"We'll have to check out all of those possibilities."
Kennedy was scribbling a mind map of circles and lines
to show how their ideas might connect.

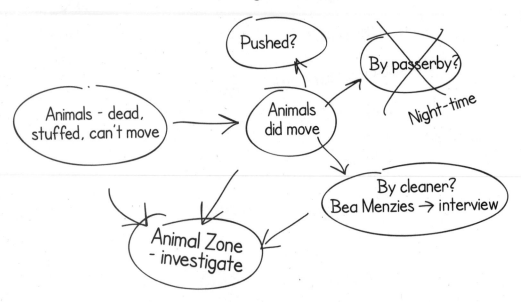

"We need to know what's been moving, how far it's gone
and who was nearby at the time."

As Kennedy wrote, Nabster checked off the essential
gadgets and handy items in his equipment bag:

Camera (+ spare memory card) ✓

ScanRay - hand scanner ✓

Mints (soft) ✓

Mints (hard) ✓

Measuring tape (electronic) ✓

Notebook ✓

Pen (black) ✓

Pen (red) ✓

Pliers ✓

String (ball of) ✓

Walkie-talkies (3) ✓

Wire (thick) ✓

Wire (thin) ✓

A banana skin (old) ✗

A crumpled tissue (used) ✗

Some of Colin's straw (smelly) ✗

Colin

Kennedy was already heading out of the door as Nabster pulled the straps tight.

It was early. The museum wasn't open yet. But for the Museum Mystery Squad it was time to get to work: unravelling the mystery of stuffed animals that moved and meeting Moth. Whoever she was.

As they left, Colin looked up. He had finally stopped performing. Acrobatics are tough when your legs are two centimetres long.

Laurie was last out, after neatly tying giant bows with his colourful laces. "Time for a rest Colin?" he said to the panting hamster. "You could learn a thing or two from stuffed animals. Just relax!"

Closing the door, Laurie wondered aloud about the Animal Zone's moving creatures. "They *couldn't* have done it themselves. *Someone* must have moved them."

Colin, of course, didn't reply.

But Laurie was right.

Chapter 3
In which Otto is
no longer standing up

Ten minutes later, the Squad were in one of the

museum's most popular rooms: the Animal Zone. This

was where visitors came face-to-face with creatures they

had only ever seen on TV wildlife programmes.

The stuffed animals were on raised display stands

behind a low railing. This meant that people could see

but not touch. Families, school groups, tourists and those

escaping the rain had the chance to 'Ooh' and 'Aah' at

beasts of all shapes and sizes. The Animal Zone was like a safe and silent tour through a safari park frozen in time.

At the 'wee beasties' end of the scale were rats, stoats and weasels. Then things got bigger with rabbits, foxes and badgers. After that there were hyenas, gazelles and zebras. The 'biggest beasties' were bears (polar and grizzly), a rhino, a giraffe and an elephant. In the middle of it all, and looking slightly out of place beside a squirrel and a stag, was the hulking figure of Moth.

"Ah, I get it now... a mam-*moth*." Laurie had finally figured out who Moth was. "Every dinosaur circus should have one."

Moth =  ✓

"Dug out of a glacier in Russia and restored to her former glory," said Nabster. "The Dinosaur Circus have given her to the museum to display for three days while they're in town."

Moth was quite a sight. She was the size of a small truck parked right in the middle of the Animal Zone. She was no ordinary small truck though, since she was

covered in a rough blanket of thick brown fur. Long

tusks, like two ski jumps, drooped down to the ground

on either side of her trunk. Above these were bulging

eyes like giant ping-pong balls.

She dwarfed the biggest wild animals that Scotland

had to offer. The otter and the stoat looked like tiny

toys scattered at her feet.

"She's huge!" said Nabster. "Imagine Colin standing beside her!"

Kennedy walked up as close as she could to the low railing and stared at Moth.

"Your eyes look like Moth's when you do that," said Laurie.

"Ha ha." Kennedy tossed her frizzy hair and retorted. "She might be stuffed but she'd run faster than *you*."

On a display board beside Moth was an article from the previous day's local newspaper. Under a headline:

FIRST MAMMOTH IN SCOTLAND SINCE ICE AGE!

was a photo of the ringmaster, Tyrone O'Saurus, smiling proudly beside Moth, and also a statement he'd made:

"We are delighted to share this wonderful creature with the people of Edinburgh while we are visiting. Take the chance to see this amazing piece of history, and do come to the remarkable Dinosaur Circus too."

For two days, people had flocked through the doors to see the woolly exhibit. Many also went to the Dinosaur Circus. When it came to advertising, it seemed that Tyrone O'Saurus was a roaring success.

Now though, there were just two people standing in

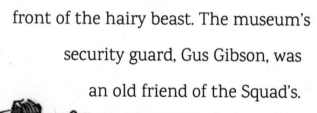

front of the hairy beast. The museum's security guard, Gus Gibson, was an old friend of the Squad's. He had been a great help in many of their previous cases. However, Gus was scratching his bald head and looking puzzled. Standing beside him and barely half his height was a small neat woman firmly holding a feather duster like a soldier in a sentry box.

"Hi guys," said Gus as the Squad approached. "We've got an odd one for you this time."

"Hi Gus," said the three children together.

"I'll say it's odd," said the woman. "In all my years of

cleaning I've never known anything like it."

Gus introduced her as Bea Menzies, the Animal Zone cleaner. Bea reached over to remove some fluff from his shoulder as he did so. Laurie took a step backwards to prevent her brushing down his top hat.

"We got an email saying there have been some strange movements," said Kennedy. "Can you tell us a bit more?"

Nabster flicked open a notepad and stood ready to write.

"Well, I've made a list," replied Bea in a businesslike manner, pulling her own piece of paper from the front pocket of her apron.

"Stevie has moved four centimetres. Donald has moved seven centimetres. But it's Otto..." Bea cleared her throat before continuing. "Otto is the most upsetting one." She looked away, fighting back tears, unable to describe what she had witnessed.

The team members glanced at each other with puzzled expressions. Gus raised his eyebrows. He had heard Bea's story already.

It was Laurie who spoke first. "Umm... who exactly are Stevie, Donald and Otto?"

Bea blinked hard and looked at Laurie as though he was daft. She could easily have got this impression from his purple kilt and top hat. But Bea was actually more shocked at his question.

"The animals of course! I've got to know them so well since I started work here a few weeks ago, I've given them all names."

Stevie was, apparently, the red squirrel. Donald was the roe deer.

"And Otto is the otter?" asked Laurie, guessing correctly.

Bea nodded. "I know every inch of their fur, teeth and claws. I also know *exactly* where they stand. Or where they *should* stand. And I can tell you that some of them are *not* where they ought to be."

"Just by a few centimetres," commented Nabster, quietly looking at Bea's notes and deciding that there was little of interest.

"Yes," said Bea. "Apart from Otto. I came in this morning and... well, look." She pointed at the animal display.

It was clear that Otto the stuffed otter normally stood up on his back legs, as if sniffing the air. Today he was lying on his back.

"He's fallen over," said Laurie flatly.

"Has he? *Has he?*" said Bea with piercing eyes. "Or was he *pushed*?"

"Why would someone push an otter over?" grumbled

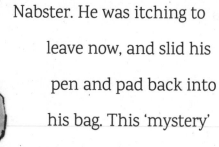

Nabster. He was itching to leave now, and slid his pen and pad back into his bag. This 'mystery' did not deserve notes.

"Have you noticed anything else strange?" Laurie asked Bea.

"Yes," said Bea seriously. "Flaky pastry."

Nabster rolled his eyes at Bea's breaking news.

"Flaky pastry?" said Kennedy in a baffled tone her teammates hadn't heard before.

"Flaky pastry," Bea repeated. She pointed to a short trail of crumbs on the floor between the mammoth and the otter.

"Well, I doubt Moth or Otto popped to the bakery for a quick sausage roll," said Kennedy.

"They couldn't eat another thing... they're *stuffed*!" Gus looked delighted with his own joke but his grin quickly faded when everyone ignored him.

"Did the crumbs appear overnight?" asked Laurie.

Bea nodded in response.

"It looks like someone has been here when they shouldn't have," said Gus.

"And they've had a midnight feast," said Kennedy. "Part of this mystery involves an intruder."

"Two questions," said Laurie. "How did they get in and what were they here for?"

Nabster reached back into his equipment bag. Perhaps there was work to be done after all.

Chapter 4
In which many
measurements are made

"We need to get some data," said Nabster, now taking

control of the situation. He pulled a camera from his

bag and snapped about 57 photos showing where the

stuffed animals stood. Bea helped Otto back to his feet in

time for his photo to be taken, dusting him down so he'd look his best.

Next Nabster took notes on which direction the animals were facing. Finally, with an electronic tape, he measured the distances between them.

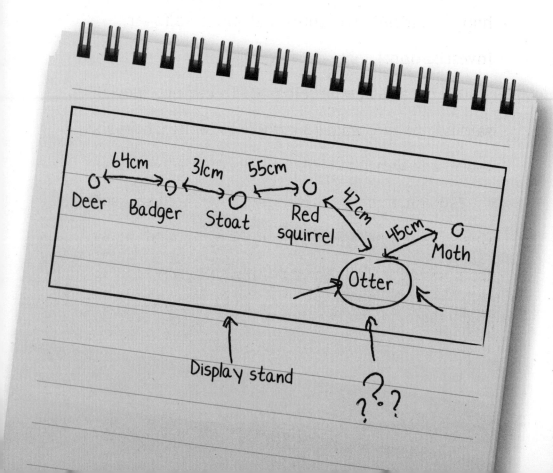

"With this we'll have an exact plan of everything," said Nabster. "If there are suspicions of anything moving again, we can compare with these measurements and be certain of what's happened."

Bea looked at her scrap of paper. She seemed happy that her own notes had started a fuller investigation.

"But that will only tell us *if* something's moved," said Laurie. "We want to know *how* stuffed animals move, and *why*."

"Well it must be this mysterious intruder," said Gus. "There's no one in the building at night apart from security staff. The cleaning shift comes in at seven o'clock. Before that the museum is deserted. Or it should be."

Laurie gave Bea one of his piercing stares through his large-framed glasses. "About these crumbs... Is your hoover working properly, Bea? Could it be spitting stuff out instead of sucking it up?"

One stern look from Bea was enough to answer that question.

Nabster rummaged in his bag again. He pulled out a gadget which looked like a supermarket hand scanner.

"The ScanRay," Kennedy observed. "Nabster's favourite bit of kit."

"I think if there was a fire in the museum, Nabster would save that gadget first, and then think about rescuing you and me," said Laurie.

"Oh, I'd get Colin before I got you two," said Nabster in a matter-of-fact voice.

He switched the scanner on and held it close to the mammoth's side.

"The age reading is going off the scale, because she's so ancient," he began.

"Careful, you might offend her!" chuckled Gus.

"Organic matter present," said Nabster. "There's metal too – must be the framework inside."

"No real surprises then," said Kennedy.

"What exactly were you expecting from a stuffed animal?" replied Laurie.

"Wait a minute. That's a bit odd," said Nabster. "I'm getting one strange reading here..."

At that moment there was a buzz of conversation

from the doorway and Museum Director Magda Gaskar arrived. Beside her was a figure the team recognised from the news coverage. The bright checked jacket was unmistakeable.

It was Tyrone O'Saurus, the Dinosaur Circus ringmaster.

Chapter 5
In which a trip to the circus is arranged

It was clear that Tyrone O'Saurus was used to making announcements in a huge tent. His voice boomed to the limit of the high ceiling. The effort of speaking so loudly led to his cheeks turning a red-going-on-purple colour, perfectly matching the blaring checks on his jacket.

"Is everything about him loud?" muttered Laurie, pulling on ear muffs as protection from the bellowing ringmaster.

Kennedy smirked but Nabster didn't appear to notice the noise. He seemed puzzled, still looking at the read-out on the ScanRay.

"Ah, here is Moth!" roared O'Saurus. "It's *so* good to see her in this wonderful building. And as ever she is pulling a crowd!" His eyes flickered around Gus, Bea and the Museum Mystery Squad, assessing his audience. He twirled the end of his tremendously curly moustache with one hand. When he let go, it whirled back like a

coiling spring. With the other hand the ringmaster toyed with a necklace that hung low over his large bowling-ball belly. The jewellery clackered and clangled as he moved it. It was made of giant fangs.

Nabster would normally have been itching to use the ScanRay on these monster teeth, but he was still distracted by his last scan.

Magda introduced everyone, briefly explaining that the team were taking the chance to see Moth. She said nothing about their investigation of unusual animal movements.

Bea was all set to tell her story again but the circus man was first to speak. "Ah, what a pleasure to meet the Museum Mystery Squad," said Tyrone O'Saurus. "Your detective skills are well known. You are almost as famous as me!" He gave a huge grin, and a thin strip of gold flashed between his two front teeth.

"Are those real?" asked Laurie, pointing at the necklace of fangs that the ringmaster was wearing.

"No, sadly not," O'Saurus replied, fingering the string of teeth. "It would be terrific if they were actual dino-dentistry. They are in fact exact copies of the fabulous ones you have here in the museum."

"The fossilised T-rex teeth? Weren't they one of the first curiosities brought to Britain from America?" said

Kennedy. She could picture the exhibit in the Fossil Zone.

"The most celebrated gnashers in Scotland," said Nabster, speaking to everyone, but still looking at his gadget.

"Not just any old teeth," said O'Saurus, waving his arms grandly. "The T-rex teeth are perfect. Still sharp enough to slay a stegosaurus today."

"Not that we find many of those in the city centre," said Laurie.

"No, they can never find a parking space!"

Nobody laughed at Gus's joke – as usual.

"Yes, we have the only complete set of T-rex teeth in the world," said Magda Gaskar proudly.

"One of our most popular exhibits. They've actually been away getting cleaned, but go back on display today."

"Excellent!" boomed Tyrone O'Saurus excitedly. "Just as I had hoped."

"Why are you so interested in the teeth?" asked Laurie.

"I visited this museum often as a child," boomed the ringmaster. (He was still talking as though there was an enormous audience, rather than six other people and thirty-four stuffed animals.) "One of the reasons I came to love dinosaurs was because of those T-rex teeth," he continued. "I used to stand in front of them for hours, imagining what it would be like to live in prehistoric times. I had dearly hoped to see them this week before the circus leaves town." He moved closer to the mammoth, his fingers still playing with his fang necklace.

58

"I'm glad you will," said Magda Gaskar. "And thank you again for lending us Moth. She's been a real bonus for the museum."

"And for us too," said O'Saurus. "It's a win-win situation." He flashed a smile and patted the mammoth. "Only one last night here my dear, so make it a good one... make it a good one."

Laurie and Kennedy glanced at each other and raised their eyebrows. The circus owner was talking to the mammoth like she was a family pet. Would he tickle her chin next and expect her to roll over?

Instead he turned to them all and his words took them by surprise. "I have a gift for you." He reached deep into his pocket. "Tickets for the last night of the Dinosaur Circus! The greatest show in town! I'm sure it must be good for you to get out of the museum now and then. I promise it will be more lively than taking measurements in a room full of stuffed animals!" O'Saurus roared with laughter.

"What a great offer!" said Magda Gaskar.

"Thanks a lot!" said Kennedy, Laurie and Nabster in unison.

On seeing the tickets, Nabster had forgotten about the ScanRay. "I'd like to see the Bronto Brothers. They look really funny."

"I'll get to see Terri Dactyl and her trapeze tricks!"

said Kennedy, clapping her hands.

"Ah, I'm afraid you'll not be able to see poor Terri," said Tyrone O'Saurus. "Unfortunately she's been a bit poorly this week. I think she ate some dodgy dino burger leftovers at our hot food stand and is still recovering. But all of the other acts will be there, I promise. And you'll have a perfect view of them from these front-row seats!" O'Saurus waved the tickets at them temptingly.

The Squad members each took one with a broad smile.

"Now I must head off," said O'Saurus. "I want to look at those amazing T-rex teeth, and then do some last-minute preparations for tonight's show. Will I see you there?"

O'Saurus seemed keen for an answer before he left, and the Squad were happy to tell him that they would definitely be at the circus that evening.

Kennedy's Diary

Monday 1.00 p.m.

We have free tickets for the Dinosaur Circus!

Despite the crazy Dino Circus names, this has made my day, since our current mystery has so little life it's nearly extinct.

We are professionals. We crack codes.

We catch criminals. We uncover secrets.

Today we looked at stuffed animals that had moved a few millimetres and considered some crumbs.

Yawn. In fact double yawn. Scrap that: make it a triple.

Laurie feels the same. He's looked out his bright orange tracksuit to cheer himself up. He'll look like a two-legged satsuma. (I've told him.)

Nabster keeps going on about his ScanRay and the idea of an intruder. He's busy on the laptop (as usual).

To do: think more about all this after Dino Circus tonight!

Nabster had been typing for ages and finished with a flourish. "Right guys," he said. "Here's what we have."

On the wall-screen, a bar chart appeared.

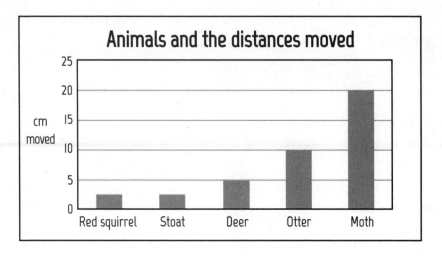

Animals and the distances moved

"Otto isn't the big story of the day. According to Bea's measurements, it's Moth who has moved the most."

Kennedy shifted her attention from her diary. "So the biggest animal has moved the furthest."

"How hard would you have to push a mammoth to make it move?" asked Laurie, staring at the ceiling and not paying much attention to Nabster's chart.

"More of a shove than a nudge," suggested Kennedy.

"I'll tell you something else that's a bit odd,"

said Nabster. "You know I said I got a strange reading on the ScanRay? Well what I found is that Moth is *warmer* than any other animal in the room."

Nabster put the results on the screen. Sure enough they showed that all of the stuffed animals were the same temperature, except for the mammoth.

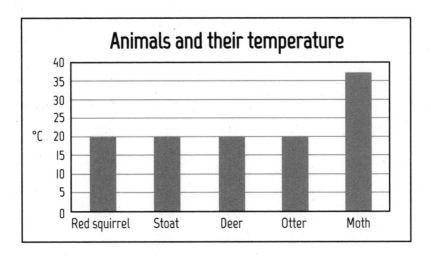

"Wait. Hold on." Kennedy was staring hard at the chart. "Moth is about the same temperature as a *live* animal."

"I know!" said Nabster. "And just to prove it, look at this." He added a final reading to the table. It was Colin's temperature. His was the same as Moth's.

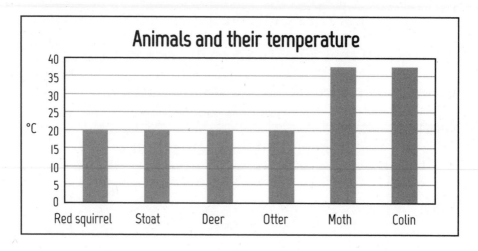

The sofa springs pinged suddenly as Laurie sat up straight. The look on his face mirrored the others: they all knew something very weird was going on.

Chapter 6
In which a radio crackles

"Go on Laurie, ask the question we're all thinking," said Nabster.

"How can a prehistoric animal, which has been dead, in fact *extinct*, for thousands of years, and was dug out of a block of *ice*, for goodness sake, be *warm*?"

"Warm and moving," added Kennedy, her eyes widening.

"You missed a bit," said Nabster. "The crumbs. This dead prehistoric animal also appears to be snacking..."

A few minutes later and the smartboard was covered

in scribbles. The three friends had created a big list:

Why Things Might Move
When They Aren't Alive

pushed

strong winds

on wheels

pulled

knocked over

sucked up
by a hoover

bumped into

driven by an engine

magnetic force fields

earthquake

exploded out
of a cannon

"I've always thought being exploded out of a cannon sounds fun," said Nabster. "But you'd need a super-big one to shift a mammoth any distance."

Laurie looked at the other items on the list. "I think we might have noticed if there had been an earthquake recently."

"Right enough," said Kennedy. "You would have rolled off the sofa."

"I think we can rule out most of that list," said Nabster. "Can you really imagine Bea hoovering clumsily between her new best friends?"

"None of the animals are on wheels," observed Kennedy. "And the last time there was a strong wind in the museum was when the window in the toilets got stuck open."

"Bea says that the animals only moved last night," said Nabster, checking his notes.

"And what else has happened in the last day or two?" Laurie posed the question.

Kennedy answered: "The circus came to town and brought Moth here."

"It's as though Moth is moving and making other things move too," said Laurie.

"Maybe she doesn't like her new home," said Nabster. "She's shuffling about, trying to get comfortable."

"Just one teensy weensy problem with that idea," said Laurie. "She's dead. As a dodo. *More* dead than a dodo, actually. Kicked the bucket. Popped her little mammothy clogs. Like about 10,000 years ago!"

Extinct 100s
of years

Extinct 1000s
of years

"But it's like she's somehow still a little bit alive," said Nabster. "She's warm. And she's leaving a trail of crumbs."

"Do you really truly think the museum has a *living mammoth* on display up there?" asked Kennedy. "It's more likely there's something wrong with your ScanRay. Maybe it's not worth rescuing in a fire after all. You can put us back at the top of your list of things to save. I think we should go back to the intruder idea. How could someone get in?"

"There's nothing wrong with the ScanRay!" Nabster was highly indignant. "I checked the temperature reading seventeen times while you were talking with Tyrone about teeth."

Laurie cut short the argument before it grew.

"We should check it again, but right now we've got a dino circus to go to and, more importantly, I can't decide whether to wear my fluffy yeti boots or the clown shoes with the fantastically long toes. Any thoughts?"

They were interrupted by a hissing crackling noise. Nabster's walkie-talkie was hanging on a peg on the door. The sound came and went like a badly tuned radio with a dodgy volume control.

"I thought I'd switched that off," said Nabster, standing up to do just that.

"**. . .Last chance. . .**" said a scratchy voice from the radio.

"Who's that speaking?" said Laurie. "It doesn't sound

like Gus." At times during their investigations the Squad used walkie-talkies to speak to each other, and also to contact Gus the security guard. He was the only other person in the building who had one. There was another burst of crackles and a distorted voice.

"**...Last chance...**" said the voice again, "**...tonight...**"

Nabster stood beside the walkie-talkie, waiting for it to say more.

After a pause, the device buzzed again.

"**...get them this time...**"

"Sounds like an advert," said Laurie. "You know, like, 'Last Chance! Tonight! Get your half-price hamster cage before it's too late!'"

Colin looked up, sniffing the air.

"It could be anyone in the city broadcasting on the same frequency," explained Nabster. "Sometimes we even pick up other people's phone calls. I remember we once heard a woman giving a shopping list to her husband who was at the supermarket: cheddar cheese, broccoli, Marmite."

"I'm glad they didn't invite me to dinner," said Laurie.

Nabster spoke into his walkie-talkie.

"Nabster to Gus. Were you trying to contact us? Over."

There was a short pause.

"Gus to Nabster. Negative. Haven't used the radio all day. Although I've been getting snippets of other people's conversations in the last day or two. Over."

"Same here. Anything interesting? Over."

"Just random words. Nothing I could make sense of. Over."

"Doesn't sound important," said Nabster. "Sorry to have disturbed you. Over and out."

Kennedy's Diary

Monday 4.00 p.m.

Plan For Tomorrow

- Check mammoth temperature reading

- Measure animal positions again

- Check for any more crumbs

- Research mammoth extinction dates

- Check doors and windows on

  Animal Zone level

- Intruder entry points?

Plan For Tonight

Dino Circus!!!

WHAT'S OLDER THAN A MAMMOTH?

| 4.54 billion | 550 million | 350 million |

REALLY OLD!

(Estimated age in years)

How old is a mammoth? Can you guess how many millions of years ago they lived? Were they alive before, or after, dinosaurs? (Answer on the last page)

 68 million

40 million

 20 million

Chapter 7
In which front-row seats aren't what they seem to be

Kennedy, Laurie and Nabster joined the crowds passing

stalls selling dino souvenirs as they headed for the giant

circus tent on the grassy Meadows. There was a babble

of excited voices. Children were carrying balloons or

wearing fossil badges. Some of them were wearing dinosaur

masks. Others had giant foam claws on their hands.

"Do you want a couple of those to add to your wardrobe?" Nabster asked Laurie, pointing at the huge fake claw hands.

"Good idea," said Laurie, taking money from the pocket of his orange trousers.

"I was only joking!" said Nabster, but Laurie ignored him and was soon wearing two huge foam dino-claw paws. In his orange suit he now looked like a satsuma crossed with a lobster.

There was a distant roar from the tent: the sound of some enormous prehistoric beast.

"Is that real?" Nabster was not the only person to look slightly concerned at the scary noise.

"Don't be daft," said Laurie. "You know there are no actual dinosaurs in the Dinosaur Circus."

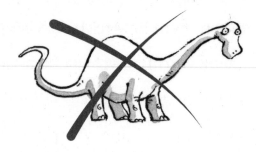

The lack of monsters didn't seem to matter to the crowd. It was growing bigger by the minute.

Kennedy showed their tickets as they filed through the jawbone archway. Inside the big top they soon found their seats.

"Brilliant!" said Nabster. "Front row and ringside! How cool is that?"

"Check out the height of this place," said Laurie. They craned their necks and looked upwards. The two enormous poles holding up the tent roof had tiny ladders with platforms at the top. There was a highwire stretched between them for Archie Opteryx to do his act.

"Shame about Terri Dactyl," said Kennedy. "It would be great to see her on the trapeze up there."

Although the circus hadn't started yet, there was plenty to keep the crowd entertained. Five acrobats were performing spectacular somersaults and ended up standing on each other's shoulders. "Colin would have got some new ideas for his hamster wheel if we'd brought him," said Nabster.

"I'll have to take these off," said Laurie removing the foam dinosaur claws. "My hands are boiling in them."

He was just in time. A juggler was getting audience members to toss balls into the air, adding to those he was already throwing round and round. Laurie caught one and chucked it back into the circular blur of objects over the juggler.

"Excellent!" said Nabster. "This is good already and it hasn't even started yet!"

Getting no response from Kennedy, Nabster turned to find that she had gone very still and was showing no excitement at all about the circus. She was staring hard, yet not really looking at anything.

"Why are we here?" Her voice was a little peculiar.

"To see the circus, stupid," said Laurie.

"With our free tickets!" grinned Nabster waving grandly at their fantastic front-row seats. "A reward for our hard work! Now cheer up. The lights are going down... It's about to begin!"

"But what if there was another reason we were given tickets?" said Kennedy, frowning from the effort of thinking hard.

"What do you mean?" asked Laurie.

"Tyrone O'Saurus said it would be good for us to get out of the museum. He said we needed something more interesting to do than *measuring stuffed animals*. But how did he even know that's what we were doing?" said Kennedy. She began to get up.

"Mmm," said Laurie thoughtfully. "You might have a point. I must admit I didn't fully trust him." He also stood up, and picked up his dino gloves.

"And I'm thinking about how things warm up. Like your hands in those crazy foam claws. And then I thought of Colin being the same temperature as Moth on the ScanRay reading," Kennedy went on. "If you hold Colin you can feel his little heart beating. That's why he's warm. What's inside heating up Moth?"

The people in the row behind were beginning to tut at the standing Squad members.

"These free tickets could be just like the dinosaur roars," said Laurie. "They get you all excited but actually they're fake."

"This seat feels pretty real to me." Nabster was desperate to see the show. "Sshh. It's starting."

Kennedy began moving along the row. "We need to get back to the museum – *now*."

"Really?" said Nabster. "Can't we just enjoy the show then go check things out?"

"Hurry!" said Kennedy.

"She's right." Laurie called along the row to Nabster: "Let's go."

With a groan Nabster followed the others, looking back at the circus ring with a pained face as he left.

"High five," said Laurie to a pair of twins he was squeezing past. They held up their hands and he popped two large foam claws onto them.

In less than a minute they were outside in the Meadows. People were now being turned away because the circus was full. "Have front-row seats. You'll love it," said Kennedy, giving their tickets to a surprised mum and two suddenly very happy children.

The Squad ran across the grass at top speed. Behind them boomed the familiar voice of Tyrone O'Saurus: **"LADIES AND GENTLEMEN, WELCOME TO THE DINOSAUR CIRCUS!"** A cheer erupted from the huge crowd. **"PREPARE TO BE AMAZED, ENTHRALLED AND INSPIRED TONIGHT!"**

"I can't see what the problem is," grumbled Nabster as he ran. "Our friendly ringmaster is still at the circus. So he's not doing anything dodgy at the museum."

89

"He doesn't have to be there. He's up to something from a distance," said Kennedy breathlessly. "Remember that walkie-talkie message we overheard?"

"I do," said Laurie. **"Last chance... Tonight... Get them."**

"We were given those tickets to make sure we wouldn't be at the museum right now," said Kennedy. "Something is about to happen there."

Chapter 8
In which there is much hiding and darkness and something lurks in the shadows

Arriving breathless at the museum, the team entered through the key-coded back door and sprinted immediately to Gus's office. It was locked.

"Maybe he's doing his evening rounds already," said Kennedy.

"Nabster calling Gus. Over." Nabster tried calling Gus's walkie-talkie three times. There was a buzz of static. "He must have switched it off," he concluded.

"Why would he have done that if he's on duty?" asked Laurie. "What's he up to?"

"Let's get to the Animal Zone," said Kennedy. "We need to check what's happening."

Moving quickly through the museum's dimly lit corridors, the three friends were soon at the entrance to the Animal Zone. By now their eyes had adjusted to the dark. Creeping around the doorframe they entered the room

where they had stood with Gus and Bea a few hours before.

They could see the shapes of familiar stuffed animals, like spooky statues in the darkness. The stag's antlers were most obvious, along with Otto, who was still upright, and the bulky outline of Moth.

Everything appeared to be normal. Nothing was moving.

Until...

They all heard a scuffing noise.

It came from behind an enormous grizzly bear on the other side of the Animal Zone. It seemed that the Museum Mystery Squad were not the only ones visiting the animals.

A tall dark figure was lurking in the shadows, taking great care not to be seen.

Had it seen them?

Kennedy tiptoed quietly backwards. Laurie ducked down. Nabster froze.

They had never breathed more quietly.

Kennedy signalled for them all to slip back out of the room, when suddenly the shadowy figure turned towards them.

A pencil-thin beam of torchlight shone at their faces.

"You lot!" There was a loud whisper.

It was Gus.

The three friends scurried over, crouching low as they ran, and squeezed beside him. They were now all in a line behind the grizzly. As hiding places go, it was a bit tight for four. They whispered a speedy explanation of why they had given up their circus tickets to get back to the Animal Zone.

It seemed that Gus had had similar thoughts. "Bea was convinced that something would happen again tonight. I didn't much like that O'Saurus guy, and those radio messages kept playing on my mind. All of that **'Last chance... Tonight...'** stuff made me suspicious."

Gus told them that he had been there for an hour already but nothing had happened.

The team settled down alongside him as best
they could, but squashed together they were far
from comfortable. For one person in particular any
excitement quickly wore off.

"I can't believe we're watching stuffed animals in the

dark instead of circus acts from front-row seats," whispered Nabster harshly. "Nothing's going to happen here."

"SSSHHH!" said Kennedy sharply, keeping a keen eye on Moth and the rest of the room. "Still no sign of anything odd."

Laurie and Gus nodded in agreement, carefully stretching their stiff limbs while staying hidden.

Ten minutes later Nabster grumbled again.

"Is there really any mystery here after all? I bet it was just Bea being dramatic with her duster."

"SSSHHH!!!" It was Laurie this time. "Why do you always get bored so quickly?" he asked.

Nabster spent five minutes trying to come up with an answer to this, but it led to him getting even more bored. He couldn't help speaking again.

"We could be watching the Bronto Brothers right now! Apparently they do this really funny thing where—"

Nabster's sentence broke off in mid-air, like a trapeze artist letting go, high over a watching crowd. When he spoke again it was in a soft, slow whisper.

"Is it just me, or is that mammoth glowing?"

Chapter 9
In which a mammoth
does something very unusual

Sure enough, there was a little circle of light on Moth's side. It moved around slowly, like a firefly.

"What's doing that?"

"Where's it coming from?"

"Why's it moving around?"

The questions came thick and fast in urgent whispers.

Gus's torch was off and Nabster wasn't using any gadgets. There were no museum lights shining onto Moth's great woolly coat.

The glow seemed to be coming from *inside* the mammoth.

Then, as suddenly as the light had appeared, it was gone.

If the light was strange, the next thing that happened was very strange indeed.

Kennedy saw it first and hissed, "Look! Look at Moth's bum!"

"It's opening up!" said Laurie.

It was true. Just like a car ferry, a large flap was lowering down from the backside of the mammoth to form a ramp.

"What on earth...?"

"Can you see inside?"

"Is that how mammoths work?"

And if that was very strange indeed, then the next thing to happen was totally weird.

An oddly shaped ball rolled down the ramp and stopped at the bottom. Then it uncurled and stood up, reaching towards the ceiling with perfectly pointed fingers like a gymnast completing a tumbling routine.

The Squad stared in disbelief. The short figure dressed in black now reached to its forehead and switched on a head torch.

Gus and the Squad ducked back tightly behind the grizzly bear.

As they hid, Kennedy whispered, "That's why Moth was glowing! The head torch! It was inside, shining out."

They all peeked back to watch what would happen next. The person moved very quickly, edging carefully between the animals, trying to avoid the sticking-out snouts and tails. But the four hidden friends noticed a badger rocking gently on its feet, brushed by the figure in black.

They nodded in agreement.

They had just seen why the stuffed animals had moved. This was the intruder, who must have rolled out of the mammoth and sneaked around the previous night too. A soft bump in the dark had been enough for

Bea to spot the difference when she arrived for work.

But two important questions remained: who was the dark figure now slipping out the door of the Animal Zone? And why were they wandering around the museum at night?

There was only one way to find out.

Follow them.

Chapter 10
In which an intruder
is tracked

Within a few seconds, the Squad and Gus were sidling

through the museum corridors in silent single file.

Crouching, and keeping close to the walls, they stayed

just out of sight of the intruder, who moved quickly,

sticking to the shadows.

On they went through a long hallway lined with swords, axes and pikes. Suits of armour stood like guards as they passed. The intruder did not pause, creeping ahead to the next room.

Following someone without being seen is not easy, but the Squad and Gus knew every inch of the museum. They could almost have walked around it with their eyes shut. (Laurie had kind of tried that once wearing a pair of enormous and extremely dark sunglasses. He had managed four corridors before falling into a display of African drums.)

This time he kept his eyes wide open.

They were soon in the Egyptian Zone, passing exhibits of jewellery and mummies once housed in pyramids. The black-clad figure moved silently onwards. Where were they going? What was their mysterious quest?

"You know what's next, don't you?" asked Laurie in a low voice.

"The Fossil Zone," said Kennedy in hushed tones. "I have a funny feeling our journey is about to end."

The doorway into the Fossil Zone was framed with two enormous dinosaur-leg pillars like bony tree trunks. Inside the room were giant slabs of rock. Even in the semi-darkness the team could see the patterns in them: fossils of leaves and branches, shells and sea creatures.

The figure glided through the room, skirting past the larger pieces, which were clearly not its target. Moments later the head-torch beam cut through the darkness, then moved around as the intruder searched for something. Round and round the room it went, light flicking and reflecting off each glass display cabinet.

Kennedy, Laurie and Nabster were positioned just behind the bony plates of a triceratops skull. It was a little trickier for Gus, who was much taller, but he stood behind the leg bone of a T-rex. At two metres, it was just longer than he was.

1.94m

2m

5-6m

Suddenly the torch beam stopped moving and the dark figure could be seen looking intently at a display case. Moments later there was a clink of tools as the intruder's tiny backpack was placed on the floor.

"What is it?" mouthed Laurie to the others. "What's in that display case?"

WHAT'S TALLER THAN A T-REX?

A T-Rex might be tall compared to a human (even one as tall as Gus!) but compared to other man-made and natural wonders it was pretty tiny!

TRUE OR FALSE?
Female T-Rex were taller than males? (Answer on the last page)

Height in metres

6 –––––

4 –––––

1.9 ––––

0.14

Colin   Gus   Mammoth   T-Rex

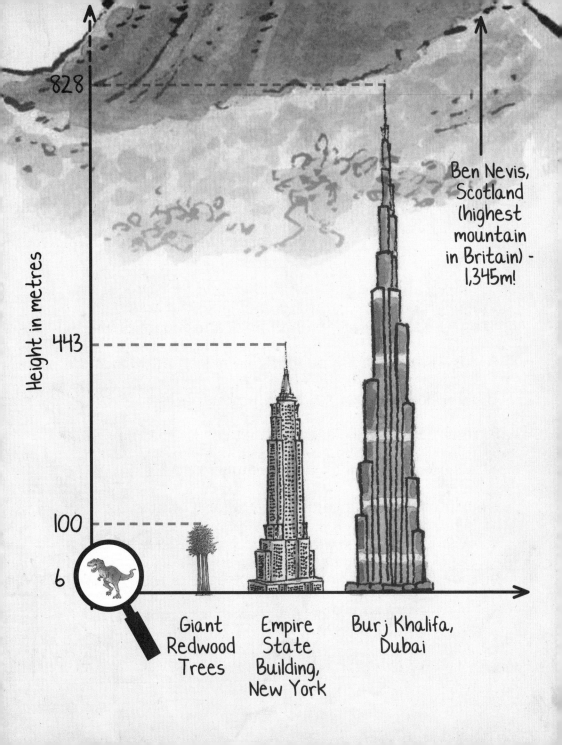

828

443

Height in metres

100

6

Giant
Redwood
Trees

Empire
State
Building,
New York

Burj Khalifa,
Dubai

Ben Nevis,
Scotland
(highest
mountain
in Britain) -
1,345m!

Chapter 11
In which thief-catching plans are hatched

Silently, Kennedy tapped her teeth and mouthed the words: "T-rex teeth." The mysterious intruder was at the display case that held the famous fangs – the ones Tyrone O'Saurus had talked about earlier that day.

The team watched for two minutes. That was all the time it took for the intruder to get what it wanted and move swiftly back the way it had come. The Squad and Gus all moved quietly around to avoid being seen, then followed once more. The return journey seemed straightforward,

as they all knew where it would end: Moth.

They arrived back in the Animal Zone just as the black figure weaved its way past Otto, who rocked on his feet, though tonight he stayed upright. The intruder tiptoed up the ramp into the mammoth. Within seconds the mammoth's bum had closed, nudging Moth half a step forward.

The room fell still, but once again animals had shifted in the night.

The Squad gathered with Gus in his office.

Laurie, typically, asked a question they were all wondering. "Do you think that thief was working alone?"

"We'll get the police to find that out," said Gus.

"Yes, but not yet, Gus, please." Kennedy's eyes were bright. "Tyrone O'Saurus was crazy about those teeth. He must be involved. And if he realises we know what's happening he'll be off like a shot. Give us until tomorrow morning, Gus. I have an idea that might let us catch our intruder *and* Tyrone red-handed."

"Go on Gus," said Nabster. "I don't think our criminal is going anywhere before morning. That thief is stuck being the stuffing inside a mammoth!"

Having persuaded him to give them a few hours, they left Gus patrolling the Animal Zone once more.

Back in the Squad HQ, Nabster pulled up information on the screen. **"The Dinosaur Circus is leaving town first thing tomorrow,"** he read from a news report.

Kennedy continued reading, **"Moth the mammoth is to re-join the circus. Crowds are expected to cheer her departure.** Right, that's what I was hoping for. Nabster, do you think you could blow something up?"

"Like balloons?"

"No, I'm not having a party. I want to make something explode!"

Kennedy's Diary

Tuesday 7.30 a.m.

I'm tired but excited. Sleep?

Me - a little.

Nabster - less than me.

Laurie - less than usual!

All of us up early and Nabster has already been busy. The HQ table is covered in wire and tape and switches. He's been snipping and sticking things onto a TV remote control like a doctor doing an operation (on a very small electronic patient)!

Laurie has of course been keeping himself busy (in between snoozes). I think he's onto his fourth change of clothes. He's looking for the perfect outfit to catch thieves in. Apparently it's dungarees and a tuxedo jacket.

Bea was here a few minutes ago. She's pleased people believe her story now. We've given her an important task to do while she's cleaning today.

Gus is itching to arrest the mystery thief right now. But he's managing to be patient and wait until we try out our plan. I just hope it works...

Bea arrived back at the HQ looking flushed. "I've done it!" she said. Her voice was high-pitched and fast with excitement. "I've put it just where you told me to," she said, looking at Nabster. "The Velcro stuck easily to Moth's fur."

"Brilliant, Bea," said Kennedy. "All we need now is for Moth's taxi to arrive!"

Thirty minutes later, Kennedy, Nabster, Laurie, Gus and Bea edged through the crowd that had gathered to watch Moth leave the city in style. All the brightly coloured Dinosaur Circus vehicles were parked along the street. There was an empty flat-bed truck at the front for the great woolly beast to lead the procession. Six sweating strongmen from the circus carried Moth triumphantly out of the museum on a wooden stretcher. They stood at the top of the steps while the crowd applauded and

Tyrone O'Saurus made a speech. He smiled, but looked like he was really in a hurry to get away.

"We are SO SORRY that Moth has to leave," he boomed. "We know she has enjoyed her short stay HUGELY. Look at the big SMILE on her face!" He played with his dinosaur fang jewellery as he roared his thanks to the museum for its generosity during the last few days.

Laurie raised an eyebrow and whispered, "*Were* they generous or did you just help yourself?"

"He's almost as fake as his necklace," said Nabster under his breath.

Then, with a farewell wave like a departing king, Tyrone O'Saurus commanded the strong men to carry Moth to the truck. People at the back of the crowd craned their necks to see.

Nabster checked and double-checked the gadget in his hand.

Bea looked ill with worry, her duster tied in a tight knot in both hands.

Laurie looked nervous.

Gus looked stern.

Kennedy looked dead certain.

"Now!" she said.

Chapter 12
In which something goes **BANG**!

Nabster hit a red button on the remote control in his hand. With a

the panel on Moth's bottom flew off!

"Good shot!" said Bea punching the air. "Take that! Woohoo! Nobody messes with my Otto and Stevie!"

There was a collective gasp from the crowd and then a short shocked pause.

Hardly daring to blink, Nabster, Laurie and Kennedy exchanged quick high fives. A thin wisp of smoke rose from a gaping hole at the mammoth's rear end as the panel of fur-covered metal smouldered on the ground.

A group of police officers briefed by Gus moved smartly towards Moth, but before they got there a bundle of black came shooting out of the creature.

It uncurled, stood up and stretched, with the sound of bones cracking.

"Terri!" gasped Tyrone O'Saurus, looking quickly around as if to check whether anyone else had noticed what just happened.

It would have been rather hard not to notice.

"Yes," said Kennedy to the others. "It's Terri Dactyl the trapeze artist. Acrobats can fold themselves up into small spaces."

"Terri!" Tyrone was in more commanding mode now, his eyes fixed on the black-clad figure. He muscled towards her like a T-rex closing in on its prey, but she ignored him and surveyed the crowd, as if she was on her high platform about to begin her act. With her hair pulled tightly back, and her hands on her hips she sported a thin smile. Then with a leap, a twirl and a triple somersault, she vaulted three rows of people.

As she did so, a black cloth bag fell to the ground.

"RAAAAH!!!!"

A raging Tyrone O'Saurus shook his fist at the nimble acrobat darting away down the street, calmly pursued by two policemen.

"Does anyone think she looks like she's suffering from food poisoning?" asked Laurie.

Tyrone bent down. He couldn't stop himself picking up the black bag and running his fingers through its contents. The real T-rex teeth. For half a second he actually looked happy.

Until, that is, the police seized the bag and put him in handcuffs.

The crowd couldn't believe what they were seeing. They pointed and chattered and took endless photos.

The Museum Mystery Squad and Gus and Bea peered into the hole at Moth's rear end to see the tiny living-space where Terri Dactyl had spent the last three days.

"A hammock inside a mammoth!" said Nabster.

"How cool is that!"

There were crumpled food wrappers from which a trail of crumbs had spilled, and equipment, including a walkie-talkie. "That's how she got her instructions from O'Saurus," said Laurie. "And that's what we heard snippets of."

"It all makes sense – **'Last chance...'**, **'Tonight...'**, **'get them'**."

Magda Gaskar joined the Squad. "Well, well, well," she said. "It seems Tyrone O'Saurus didn't just want to look at the museum's dinosaur teeth. He wanted to hang them around his own neck. Huge thanks to the Museum Mystery Squad! It's amazing what you uncovered when you started looking at a few stuffed animals."

"What will happen to Moth now?" asked Laurie.

"I think if we move some of the animals a little bit more than they shifted in the last two nights, we might find her a home here for good," said Magda.

Meanwhile, Bea was fussing over the mammoth. "Oh dear, oh dear, you poor creature. You need to be patched up. Very undignified to have your... your..."

"Your bottom blown off in front of a large crowd?" said Laurie.

Bea looked a bit embarrassed. "Yes, yes, I suppose that's what I meant."

Last Chapter
In which the Case is Closed

Later, back in the HQ, Nabster was completing some notes and closing the file on the Case of the Moving Mammoth. Kennedy was writing in her diary. Laurie was a lump in a sleeping bag on the sofa. Only a cap with a propeller on it stuck out. Busier than all of them was Colin. He was doing new stunts in his cage. Nabster had connected his hamster wheel to a row of tiny coloured bulbs, and Colin was running fast enough to set off red, green and orange flashes like traffic lights gone crazy.

"Who needs a circus when you've got Colin?" said Kennedy.

"You can rely on him for a good performance."

"And the only thing he'd try and steal is some carrots," said Nabster.

"It will be quieter round here without O'Saurus roaring his head off," said Kennedy.

"He won't be missed," said Nabster. "Though Laurie might long for some more bad dinosaur puns."

There was no reaction from the figure on the sofa, just the sound of very deep breathing.

"What do you call a prehistoric creature in a sleeping bag?" asked Nabster.

Kennedy looked blank and shrugged.

Nabster grinned. "A dino-snore!"

"Ha ha," said Laurie's muffled voice.

Mike Nicholson

Mike Phillips

Mike Nicholson is a bike rider, shortbread baker, bad juggler and ear wiggler, and author of the *Museum Mystery Squad* series among other books for children.

Mike Phillips learnt to draw by copying characters from his favourite comics. Now he spends his days drawing astronauts, pirates, crocodiles and other cool things.

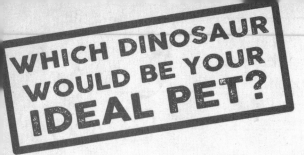

WHICH DINOSAUR WOULD BE YOUR IDEAL PET?

Start here!

Do you want a dinosaur pet that eats animals?

NO

Do you want your dinosaur pet to have TWO BRAINS?

YES

STEGOSAURUS

NO

Do you want a pet that is larger than an elephant?

YES

BRONTOSAURUS

NO

TRICERATOPS

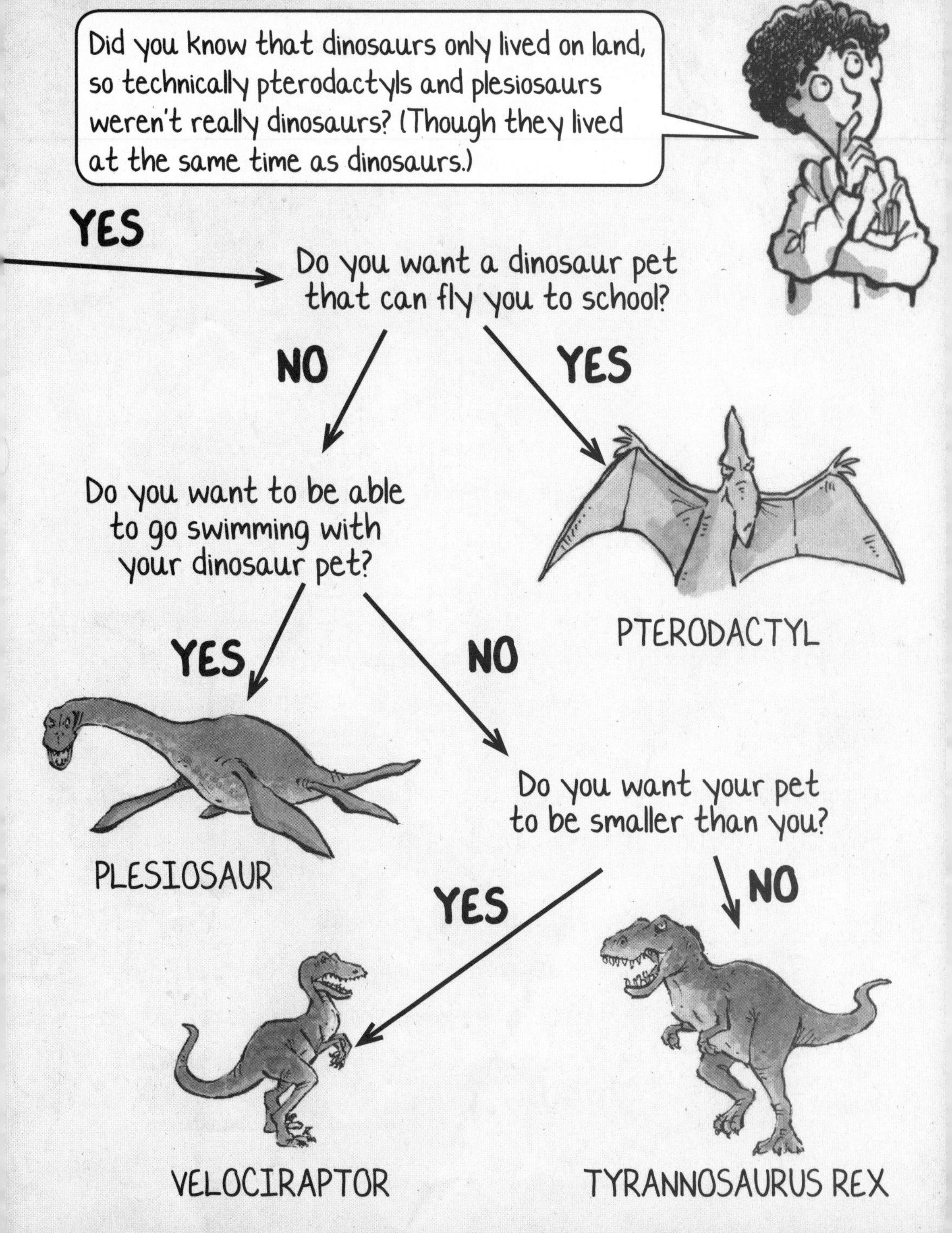
Did you know that dinosaurs only lived on land, so technically pterodactyls and plesiosaurs weren't really dinosaurs? (Though they lived at the same time as dinosaurs.)
YES
Do you want a dinosaur pet that can fly you to school?
NO
YES
PTERODACTYL
Do you want to be able to go swimming with your dinosaur pet?
YES
NO
PLESIOSAUR
Do you want your pet to be smaller than you?
YES
NO
VELOCIRAPTOR
TYRANNOSAURUS REX

Mostly As - You're Kennedy!

You have tonnes of energy and no one can keep up with you. You love to write in your diary and you're super smart.

Mostly Bs - You're Nabster!

You have a knack for creating things. And for taking things apart. You love history but you also couldn't live without the latest gadget.

Mostly Cs - You're Laurie!

You're a wacky person with seriously cool style. You're so laid back you're horizontal (literally!) because you love nothing more than a good snooze. You know how to ask the right questions.

Mostly Ds - You're Colin!

You're a hamster! You're small, furry and full of attitude (or should that be carrots?!) You're happy being exactly who you are - the coolest, cleverest member of the Squad.

More answers

p.79   Mammoths lived about 5 million years ago, after giraffes but long before humans.

p.110   True. They had to be bigger and heavier to protect their eggs from predators.